1

P

Dy

This book belongs to:

_____

For little Milly, who has only just arrived
but is already sprinkling her magic. M.B.

To my brother Oscar, who showed
me there is magic everywhere. A.S.

FAR
FAR
AWAY
BOOKS

Stardragon

Moira Butterfield   Adolfo Serra

One starry evening a little boy called Alfie
learned that there is magic in the world.

A baby blue dragon flew down, and with one flick of
his tail he turned into a kitten, right before Alfie's very eyes.

Meow!

"I've found a dragoncat,"
Alfie excitedly told Mum. But Mum just smiled.

Mum didn't notice the tiny blue dragon
flame that flickered for a second from
the kitten's nose and then disappeared.

"You can look after him until we find
out where he comes from,"
she said, walking back into the house.

"You flew down from the stars, didn't you?"
Alfie whispered to his new friend.

"I am going to call you Stardragon."

That night, Alfie sang Stardragon a lullaby.

"Twinkle, twinkle little star.
A dragoncat is what you are."

Nobody knew Stardragon's secret but Alfie.

The next morning, Barney the dog popped
his head over the fence and barked loudly.

Ruff, ruff!

Stardragon jumped.
His whiskers went blue.
His paws and his claws went
blue, and he turned into a dragon
right before Alfie's very eyes.

"I've got a dragoncat," Alfie told Dad. But with one flick of his tail Stardragon became a kitten again.

Dad didn't notice the shiny blue wings that fluttered for a second on the kitten's shoulders and then disappeared.

And still nobody knew Stardragon's secret but Alfie.

When Alfie's sister Mel
came home from school,
she accidentally slammed
shut the kitchen door.

Bang!

Stardragon jumped.
His whiskers went blue.
His paws and his claws went blue,
and he turned into a dragon right
before Alfie's very eyes.

"We've got a dragoncat," Alfie told Mel. But with one flick of his tail Stardragon became a kitten again.

Mel didn't notice the wavy dragon frill that shivered for a second down the kitten's back and then disappeared.

And **still** nobody knew Stardragon's secret but Alfie.

Alfie's new kitten became a dragon whenever something made Stardragon jump.

When he heard a wasp buzzing around the flowerbed, or saw a fox prowling past the gate.

And even once, quite by accident, when he sneezed!

Atchoo!

And **still** nobody knew Stardragon's secret but Alfie.

People shook their heads when Alfie told them what Stardragon would do.

"There are no such things as dragoncats," they said, tut-tutting.

One evening, Stardragon did
nothing but stare at the stars
in the night sky. Alfie could see
that his new friend was very sad.

"When you first landed in our
garden, I think you were
learning to fly and you
got lost. Is that right,
Stardragon?" asked Alfie.

"Do you miss your mum?
I would miss my mum."

Stardragon just kept staring at the stars.

Alfie had a good idea.

"I'll wish upon the stars for you," he said,

then he pointed to the sky and called out...

I wish upon the stars
so bright.
Please bring
Stardragon's mother
here tonight.

Almost as soon as the words had
left Alfie's mouth, a cat sprang from
the branches of the apple tree and
landed gently right in front
of Stardragon.

The orange and white cat wrapped
her furry tail around Stardragon
and they rubbed their velvety
cat noses together.

"Are you a dragoncat just like Stardragon?"
Alfie asked eagerly.

The cat turned to Alfie and purred.

"Nobody here believes that dragoncats
really exist... but I do," said an excited Alfie.

"I wish they did, then they would see
how wonderful dragoncats are."

Stardragon's mother stared at Alfie
with her round, golden eyes. Then she
looked up at the stars and began to sing.

Alfie could hear the words because he
believed in magical things.

" Come down, dragoncats.
Come down, dragoncats."

Then, from far beyond the Milky Way, came dragoncats of every colour of the rainbow.

Alfie's family ran outside and, at last,
they saw that he had been right all along.

If dragoncats are real
(and very wonderful),
then there really is magic
in the world if you look.

But you knew that
already, didn't you?

The End

First published in Great Britain in 2013
by
Far Far Away Books and Media Ltd.
20-22 Bedford Row, London. WC1R 4JS

ISBN 978-1-908786-75-3 (Hardback)
ISBN 978-1-908786-37-1 (Paperback)

A CIP catalogue record for this book is available from the British Library.

Designed at www.aitchcreative.co.uk
Edited by Richard Trenchard.

Printed and bound in Portugal by Printer Portuguesa.

All Far Far Away Books can be ordered from
www.centralbooks.com

www.farfarawaybooks.com